Humphrey's Tiny Tales

My Summer Fair SURPRISE!

Betty G. Birney worked at Disneyland and the Disney Studios, has written many children's television shows and is the author of over twenty-five books, including the bestselling *The World According to Humphrey*, which won the Richard and Judy Children's Book Club Award, *Friendship According to Humphrey*, *Trouble According to Humphrey*, *Surprises According to Humphrey* and *More Adventures According to Humphrey*. Her work has won many awards, including an Emmy and three Humanitas Prizes. She lives in America with her husband.

Humphrey's Tiny Tales

My Summer Fair SURPRISE!

BETTY G. BIRNEY

Illustrated by Penny Dann

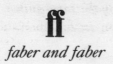

faber and faber

First published in 2011
by Faber and Faber Limited
Bloomsbury House,
74–77 Great Russell Street,
London WC1B 3DA

Printed in England by CPI Bookmarque, Croydon

A CIP record for this book
is available from the British Library

ISBN 978–0–571–24631–1

2 4 6 8 10 9 7 5 3 1

Welcome to MY WORLD

Hi! I'm Humphrey. I'm lucky to be the classroom hamster in Room 26 of Longfellow School. It's a big job because I have to go home with a different student each weekend and try to help my friends. Luckily, my cage has a lock-that-doesn't-lock, so I can get out and have BIG-BIG-BIG adventures!

I'd like you to meet some of my friends

Og

a frog, is the other classroom pet in Room 26. He makes a funny sound: BOING!

Mrs Brisbane

is our teacher. She really understands her students – even me!

Lower-Your-Voice-A.J.

has a loud voice and calls me Humphrey Dumpty.

Wait-For-The-Bell-Garth

is A.J.'s best friend and a good friend of mine, too.

Golden-Miranda

has golden hair, like I do. She also has a dog named Clem. Eeek!

Speak-Up-Sayeh

is unsqueakably smart, but she's shy and doesn't like to speak in class.

Aldo Amato

is a grown-up who cleans Room 26 at night. He's a special friend who always brings me a treat and seems to understand my squeaks better than most humans.

Repeat-It-Please-Richie

is Aldo's nephew and a classmate of mine.

I think you'll like my other friends, too, such as *Stop-Giggling-Gail, Pay-Attention-Art, Raise-Your-Hand-Heidi* and *Sit-Still-Seth.*

CONTENTS

Surprising News

I've learned a lot about school in the short time I've lived in one.

As a classroom hamster, I get to see and hear everything that goes on in Room 26.

One thing I've learned is that it's important to listen to our teacher.

Mrs Brisbane is unsqueakably smart. She's a good teacher, too.

I've also learned that it's important to listen to the headmaster, Mr Morales.

Mr Morales is the Most Important Person at Longfellow School.

One Monday when he came into our classroom, he said something *very* important.

It was also quite surprising.

'As you know, class, the Longfellow School Summer Fair is coming up on Saturday,' he said.

My friends got very excited.

'WILL THERE BE CAKE?' A.J. asked.

A.J.'s voice is very loud, so I call him Lower-Your-Voice-A.J.

Mr Morales said there would be cake.

There would also be games and crafts and things that sounded like FUN-FUN-FUN.

'Yippee!' I shouted.

Of course, all that my friends heard was a very loud 'Squeak!'

'This year, we're trying to raise money for new playground equipment. We're adding something new,' Mr Morales said. 'And you will all be part of it.'

'Are you listening, Og?' I squeaked to my neighbour.

Og is a frog. He lives in a tank right next to my cage on a long table by the window.

Since I can't see his ears, I'm never sure if he's listening or not.

'BOING-BOING!' he answered in his funny voice.

I guess he was listening
after all.

'The students in each
room are going to do a
project about what they
like best about their class.
Everyone will make posters
and banners,' Mr Morales
explained.

'Oooh,' my classmates said.

'Then, in the afternoon, all classes will parade their banners around the school field,' Mr Morales said. 'There will be a prize for the best class presentation.'

'Ahhh,' my classmates said.

'Do you think Room 26 will win?' Mrs Brisbane asked the class.

Every student shouted 'Yes!' including me.

After Mr Morales left, Mrs Brisbane talked to the class about maths.

I was so excited, I hopped on my wheel for a fast spin.

I should have listened to Mrs Brisbane, but all I could think about was the fair.

'It sounds exciting, doesn't it, Og?' I asked when we were alone during breaktime.

'BOING-BOING!' Og answered.

'Cake tastes yummy. And games are fun!' I squeaked.

'BOING-BOING-BOING!' Og agreed.

'I just have one question, Og. Do you think Room 26 will win the prize?' I asked.

Og dived into the water and splashed loudly.

I guess he wasn't sure.

I wasn't sure, either. But I knew we'd find out VERY-VERY-VERY soon.

★

I heard my friends say some very odd things when they came back from break.

'Coconuts,' Garth said.

Gail giggled and said, 'Sponges!'

Stop-Giggling-Gail loves to giggle, but I had never heard her laugh about sponges before.

Sayeh, who I call Speak-Up-Sayeh because she hardly ever speaks, smiled and said, 'Face painting!'

Face painting – what was that?

I hoped she was talking about
paintings *of* faces.

Painting *on* faces would be VERY-
VERY-VERY messy.

Especially on a hamster.

'Class, it's time to start our project,' Mrs Brisbane announced.

'We need to think about our posters. What do you like best about our class?' she asked.

Lots of hands went up.

'We learn a lot of important things in Room 26,' Mandy said.

I had to agree with that.

I've even learned to read and write in Room 26, which is unusual for a hamster.

'We've got the best teacher,' Richie said.

That made Mrs Brisbane smile.

'But other classes have good teachers and learn a lot. Any other ideas?' she asked.

I looked around the room.

I liked the unsqueakably nice bulletin board with pictures of important people on it.

I didn't know who the people were, but I was sure they were important.

I looked around some more and saw books, pencils, paper and maps.

My friends glanced around the room, too.

Then Miranda Golden raised her hand. I think of her as Golden-Miranda because of her golden hair.

'We have the nicest students,' she said with a smile. 'And the best friends.'

She was RIGHT-RIGHT-RIGHT! I was lucky to be in a class with such nice humans. 'I agree,' Mrs Brisbane said.

Suddenly, Heidi said, 'I like
Humphrey and Og!'

(Heidi doesn't always remember to
raise her hand before speaking. That's
why I call her Raise-Your-Hand-
Heidi.)

Then A.J. shouted, 'They're what I

like best about Room 26!'

Suddenly, the class was buzzing with excitement.

Mrs Brisbane clapped her hands to quieten everyone down.

'Quiet, please,' she said. 'I agree. Humphrey and Og make this class very special. We could put pictures of them on our posters for the parade.'

My classmates all cheered but I was too surprised to squeak up.

I've been a classroom hamster for quite a while.

But I'd NEVER–NEVER–NEVER had my picture on a parade poster before.

★

On Tuesday, Mrs Brisbane gave each student a large piece of cardboard.

'It's time to start making our posters,' she said.

My friends all went to work drawing and writing on the blank pieces of cardboard.

They couldn't finish them in one day, because they still had lessons to do as well.

So the next day, Wednesday, they worked on the signs again.

By the end of the day, I could finally see what they had done.

Richie's sign read: *Room 26 is hamster-iffic!*

Art's sign read: *Room 26 is frog-tastic!*

I think they meant that Og and I were terrific and fantastic.

That made me feel GOOD-GOOD-GOOD.

There were other great signs, too. Miranda's read: *Humphrey rules!*

Sayeh's sign said: *Go, Og!* That's funny, because Og is 'go' spelled backwards.

Tabitha and Kirk made signs that read: *Hamster Power* and *Frogs Rule!*

The signs were every colour of the rainbow.

Some had flowers and glitter.

Some had funny pictures of Og and me.

All of them made me proud to be in Room 26!

*

The next day, after science, my friends made ears.

YES-YES-YES! They took paper, scissors, crayon and glue and made little hats with hamster ears sticking up.

It was unsqueakably funny to see my human friends wearing hamster ears.

(They didn't
make frog ears
because, as I said,
frogs don't have
ears that you can
see.)

'You've done a
wonderful job,' Mrs
Brisbane told the
class. 'Tomorrow
we'll practise our
marching.'

★

I didn't wait
until the next
day to work on
my marching.

Once my classmates had gone home, I started to practise.

'One-two-three-four.' I marched across my cage.

'One-two-three-four.' I marched back across my cage again.

I heard Og splashing around in his tank.

Splashing was not like marching.

But frogs weren't like hamsters, either.

*

'Aldo's here to bring you cheer!' a friendly voice said later that evening.

Aldo, the school caretaker, wheeled his cleaning trolley into the room.

'How are my favourite classroom pets?' he asked.

'Unsqueakably fine!' I answered.

'BOING!' Og said.

Aldo glanced around the room and saw Richie's jacket still draped over his chair.

'Oh-oh. Richie forgot his jacket,' he said. 'I'll have to talk to him about that.'

Aldo happens to be Richie's uncle.

As usual, Aldo went right to work. While he swept and dusted, he talked to us.

'Guess what, fellows?' he asked.

'What?' I squeaked back.

'I'm going to be in the wet-sponge booth for the fair,' he said.

I was squeakless.

Gail had said something about sponges. But what on earth was a wet-sponge booth?

'Yep. People pay money to throw wet sponges at some of the folks who work at the school,' he said. 'I think even Mr Morales is going to have sponges thrown at him.'

I couldn't imagine anyone throwing a sponge at the headmaster *or* the caretaker.

'Anything to help make money for the new playground equipment,' he said.

I could see his point, but I hoped no one would throw a wet sponge at me. After all, hamsters should NEVER-NEVER-NEVER get wet!

Og probably wouldn't mind, since he spent half his time in the watery part of his tank.

When Aldo finished cleaning, I

practised marching some more.

I didn't know much about fairs, but I knew one thing: I was going to be unsqueakably good at marching!

It's Not Fair!

On Friday, Mrs Brisbane announced that it was time to finish the signs for the parade. She had brought long sticks so the students could hold them up.

Once the sticks were attached to the signs, my friends marched around the classroom, carrying them.

'One-two-three-four,' I squeaked as

I marched across my cage.

'The signs look wonderful,' Mrs Brisbane said. 'Hold them high.'

'Shouldn't we do something else?' Raise-Your-Hand-Heidi said.

'Like what?' Mrs Brisbane asked.

Heidi wasn't sure but Speak-Up-Sayeh had an idea.

'We could say something about Room 26,' she said softly.

Garth said, 'Yeah. Something about Humphrey and Og.'

That idea got my whiskers wiggling!

Soon, all my

friends were making up sayings
about Room 26.

Humphrey-Humphrey, Og-Og!
We've got a hamster and a frog!'
And:
BOING-BOING, SQUEAK-
SQUEAK,
Humphrey and Og — hear them speak!
But they finally decided on:
Humphrey and Og are so much fun,
They make our classroom number 1!

★

My friends marched around the
classroom again, chanting about Og
and me.

I was so excited, I squeaked along
with them.

Humphrey and Og are so much fun,
They make our classroom number 1!
It was paw-sitively thrilling!

Mrs Brisbane finally stopped the marching and my friends sat back down.

'Thank you for such good work,' she said. 'At the fair tomorrow, you can have fun with your friends and families until 2 p.m. Then we'll all meet by the bouncy castle and line up for the parade.'

A castle that bounces? How could that be?

Garth raised his hand. 'Who will bring Humphrey and Og?' he asked.

Mrs Brisbane looked surprised.

'Bring them where?' she said.

'Bring them out for the parade,' Garth said.

Mandy, Miranda and Richie all raised their hands and offered to bring us.

Mrs Brisbane shook her head.

'I'm sorry,' she said. 'Humphrey and Og can't be in the parade. It would be too dangerous.'

I could see how sorry my friends were. But no one was more disappointed than I was.

Og dived down into the bottom of his tank. I think he was upset, too.

Golden-Miranda asked why it
would be dangerous.

Mrs Brisbane explained that I was
too small to march in a parade and
if someone carried me, I might get
hurt.

She said that Og certainly couldn't
march and he needed to be near
water.

She also said that it was going to
be a hot, sunny day. The hot sun is
not good for hamsters or for frogs.

Everything she said was true, but I
still felt SAD–SAD–SAD.

So did my friends.

'Maybe we could pull them in a
trolley,' Garth suggested.

Now that was an unsqueakably good idea!

'There's still the sun,' Mrs Brisbane said. 'I would worry about Humphrey and Og.'

'They could wear hats,' Stop-Giggling-Gail said. Then she giggled.

Everyone else giggled, too.

I guess a hamster would look pretty funny wearing a hat.

'I know!' Mandy said. 'He could have an umbrella.'

Everyone giggled at the thought of a hamster holding an umbrella, too.

'I'm sorry,' Mrs Brisbane said. 'I don't think Humphrey and Og can be in the parade. But everyone will know about them because of your signs.'

She moved on to talking about

maps and faraway places.

I moved on to thinking about the fair.

The fair I would never ever see.

*

I always look forward to going home with a different student each weekend.

So I was surprised when Mrs Brisbane told me I would spend the night in the classroom.

'Everyone in class will be coming to the fair tomorrow morning,' she said. 'You'd be left alone all day in someone's house if they took you home tonight. After the fair, I'll take you to my house.'

I was still disappointed I wouldn't
be going to the fair.

But I'd had lots of good times at
the Brisbanes' house.

'Fine with me!' I squeaked.

★

Aldo came back to clean that night.

I didn't even know he cleaned on
Friday nights!

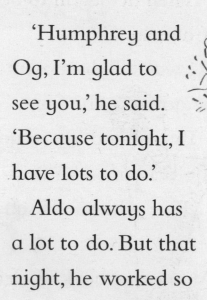

'Humphrey and
Og, I'm glad to
see you,' he said.
'Because tonight, I
have lots to do.'

Aldo always has
a lot to do. But that
night, he worked so

fast it made my head spin.

When the room was clean, he said,
'I'm not finished yet.'

Then he began to behave very
strangely.

First, Aldo measured my cage.
He'd never done that before.

Next, he measured Og's tank.
He certainly hadn't done that
before.

'Aldo, what are you doing?' I squeaked.

'Hang on, Humphrey,' he answered. 'You'll find out what's going on soon enough.'

Aldo measured the top of his cleaning trolley.

He made some notes on a piece of paper.

'Great,' he said. 'Everything will be finished in time for the fair tomorrow.'

'WHAT-WHAT-WHAT are you squeaking about?' I asked.

Aldo didn't answer. He wheeled his cleaning trolley out the door.

'What was that all about, Og?' I asked.

Og didn't answer. I guess he didn't know either.

Humans often did odd things.

But the fair made humans act even stranger than usual!

My BIG-BIG-BIG Surprise

The next morning, I woke up in Room 26. But it wasn't like any school day I'd ever known.

First, when Mrs Brisbane unlocked the door, her husband was with her.

'I can't wait to show you the posters,' she told him.

While Mrs Brisbane went to get them, Mr Brisbane rolled his

wheelchair over to see Og and me.

'Hi, fellows,' he said.

'Good morning,' I squeaked.

When Mr Brisbane saw the signs, he said my friends had done a great job.

'Yes,' Mrs Brisbane said. 'But they'll be disappointed if they don't win.'

Mr Brisbane tried on a hamster-ear hat and looked unsqueakably funny.

Next, A.J. and Garth

rushed in. They were SO-SO-SO
excited.

'Richie said to meet him here,' A.J.
said. 'He said it was important.'

'I haven't seen him yet,' Mrs
Brisbane told him.

Sayeh and Miranda hurried into the
room.

'Richie said to meet him here,'
Miranda said. 'He said he had
something to show us.'

Soon, most of my classmates were in
Room 26, all looking for Richie.

But Richie still wasn't there.

'I hope he comes soon,' Mandy said.
'I don't want to miss the face painting.'

Just as everyone was about to give

up, the door opened and Richie
entered.

Aldo was right behind him, pushing
his cleaning trolley.

Did Aldo clean on Saturdays, too?

'Wait till you see what Uncle Aldo
made,' Richie said.

Everyone gathered around Aldo and
the trolley, even Mr and Mrs Brisbane.

Of course, I couldn't see very well
from the table by the window.

I climbed up to the tippy-top of
my cage to get a better look.

'I thought of a way that
Humphrey and Og can march with
you,' Aldo said.

'Really?' I squeaked.

'Would you like to see how?' Aldo
asked.

'Oh, yes,' Mrs Brisbane said, and
everyone agreed.

Aldo came over to the window and
picked up my cage.

'I'll be careful with you, Humphrey.'

He gently placed my cage on a
board he put across the top of the

trolley. He set my cage in slots on the board.

'I fixed it so his cage won't slide around,' Aldo said.

'Very clever,' Mr Brisbane said, and everyone agreed.

Next, Aldo got Og's tank and put it in another set of slots on the board.

'Og's tank will stay firmly in place,' Aldo said.

'BOING!' Og said. He sounded very happy.

'Yes, but what about the hot sun?' Mrs Brisbane asked.

Aldo took out a big umbrella and put the handle in another slot on the board.

'They'll be in shade the whole
time,' he said. 'What do you think?'

Of course, my friends thought it
was a GREAT-GREAT-GREAT
idea.

But Mrs Brisbane was the teacher. It was up to her.

'I think it will be fine for Humphrey and Og to march with us,' she said. 'Thank you, Aldo.'

'THANKS-THANKS-THANKS, Aldo!' I squeaked.

Everybody laughed.

'I think we're ready for the fair,' Mrs Brisbane said.

He was right. I was READY-READY-READY to go.

*

The hallway whizzed by us as Aldo rolled the trolley down the hall.

Mr Brisbane rolled along next to us.

'Hey, Og, we're going to the fair!' I
squeaked.

I could hardly believe it.

Aldo rolled us through the
doorway, out to the playground.

I'd only seen the playground once before.

I'd seen swings and a slide and lots of open space.

But today, the playground looked completely different.

'What do you think, fellows?' Aldo asked as he pushed us through the crowd.

What did I think? I thought it was amazing!

The open space was filled with people and the most wonderful sights I'd ever seen.

I looked to my right and saw Garth throwing balls at a row of coconuts.

One of the balls knocked the
coconut off its base and everybody
cheered.

'Yay, Garth!' I squeaked.

I doubt if anyone heard me over
all the other noise.

I looked to my right and saw a

table filled with cakes of every size,
shape and colour. Yum!

We moved along and I saw a huge
green castle with children bouncing
up and down inside.

'That must be the bouncy castle,' I
said. 'It looks like fun, doesn't it, Og?'

Og just stared at the crowds with
his big frog eyes.

Mrs Brisbane came up with a

small tiger by her side.

At least I thought it was a tiger.

But it turned out to be Sayeh,
painted to look like a tiger.

'I got my face painted,' she said
with a happy smile.

I still wasn't interested in getting
my face painted.

But it would be fun to be a tiger, at least for a day.

Aldo said he had to go to the wet-sponge booth, so Mrs Brisbane said she'd push the trolley.

'I don't want to miss this,' she said.

She wheeled us past more booths and tables, with games and yummy things to eat.

There was a big crowd gathered around the next booth.

Everyone was laughing at something. But I couldn't see what it was.

'I'll have a look, Og,' I shouted to my friend.

I climbed up to the tippy-top of

my cage, where I hung from one
paw.

I saw a big board with a hole in
it. Sticking out through the hole was
Mr Morales's head!

I was astonished to see my friend,
Golden-Miranda, toss a wet sponge
right at his face.

Splat! The sponge hit him
in the forehead and water
rolled down Mr Morales's
face.

I was SHOCKED-
SHOCKED-SHOCKED
that anyone would treat
the headmaster like that.

Especially a nice girl like
Miranda.

But the most amazing
part was that Mr Morales
was laughing!

'Who's next?' he shouted.

'It's all for a good cause. We're raising money for new playground equipment.'

So what looked like a very bad thing turned out to be a very good thing.

'Should I give it a try?' Mrs Brisbane asked.

'Sure,' Mr Brisbane answered. 'He said it's for a good cause.'

I never thought I'd see the day

when my teacher would throw a wet
sponge at my headmaster. But she
did.

As the crowd cheered, she pulled
her arm back and let the sponge fly.

It hit him right on the nose.

Everybody laughed. Mr Morales
laughed the loudest.

Summer fairs were fun, all right.

They were also very surprising.

I Surprise Everybody

Mr Morales had to leave the booth to get ready for the parade. Aldo took his place.

The first person to buy a ticket to throw a sponge was Richie.

He pulled his arm way back and threw it at his uncle.

Splat! It hit Aldo on the side of his head.

He laughed so hard, his moustache
shook.

'You can do better than that,
Richie,' he said. 'Try again.'

Meanwhile, Mrs Brisbane went to
get the signs for our class.

She left Miranda in charge of Og
and me.

'It's almost time, Humphrey,'
Miranda said as she wheeled us
towards the bouncy castle.

I watched all the children bouncing
around inside.

My tummy felt a little bouncy, too.

Soon Mrs Brisbane was back,
handing out signs to all my friends.

'Look at me, Humphrey,' someone
said.

I looked up and saw a giant
hamster. Eeek!

'It's me – Seth,'
the giant hamster
said. 'I had my
face painted like a
hamster!'

I was HAPPY-HAPPY-HAPPY to
see that it really was Seth.

'Look at me,' another voice said.

I looked up and saw a huge green
face.

'It's me –
Tabitha,' the green
face said. 'I had
my face painted
like a frog!'

'BOING-BOING!' Og said. He
sounded quite pleased.

My classmates were all lined up
now, holding their signs.

They looked unsqueakably fine
wearing their hamster-ear hats.

Mrs Brisbane told the students to

march in two straight lines, holding
their signs high.

'When we get to the stage,
A.J., you lead the chant,' she said.
'Everyone will be able to hear you.'

She asked Miranda and Richie to
push the trolley together.

'I've got an idea,' Richie said.

I couldn't hear what it was because
he whispered it to Miranda.

As the classes lined up, I saw
children carrying all kinds of
colourful signs and banners.

My tummy did a flip-flop. Would Room 26 be the best after all?

'Eek!' I squeaked.

But no one could hear me because a band began to play loud music.

'All right, students. Forward, march!' Mrs Brisbane said.

The trolley lurched forward.

'Og, we're in a parade!' I told my froggy friend.

'BOING-BOING-BOING-BOING!' he replied.

As we marched along, mums and dads, brothers, sisters and grandparents waved at us and cheered us on.

'Signs high! Here we go, A.J.!' Mrs Brisbane said.

We stopped marching when we
reached a wooden stage on the edge
of the playing field.

'Okay, Humphrey,' Richie said.
'I've got a plan for you that will

surprise everybody. Even Mrs
Brisbane doesn't know.'

I was surprised when he opened
the door to my cage.

I was surprised when he pulled my

hamster ball out of his backpack and put me inside.

Richie set my hamster ball on the ground.

'Now you can march, Humphrey,' he said.

Mrs Brisbane looked surprised, too.

'Richie!' she said. 'I don't think that's a good idea.'

I looked UP-UP-UP and saw Mr Morales and some other people sitting on the stage, watching.

I heard A.J.'s loud voice lead the others.

Humphrey and Og are so much fun,
They make our classroom number 1!

They sounded great.

I sat in my hamster ball, listening.

'Go, Humphrey, go!' Richie yelled.

I'd forgotten he'd told me to march.

I took a few steps forward, which made my ball spin.

'Go, Humphrey, go!' the whole class shouted.

'No, Humphrey, no!' Mrs Brisbane said.

I suddenly hit a little slope and my ball rolled a little faster.

'Go, Humphrey, go!' the whole crowd yelled.

The slope got steeper and steeper.

My ball rolled faster and faster.

Large feet moved out of the way to let me pass as I rolled along.

I was moving FAST-FAST-FAST. Faster than I'd ever gone before.

'Whoa, Humphrey! Come back!' Richie shouted.

I heard footsteps running behind me.

My ball just kept on going.

'Stop, Humphrey, stop!' I heard the crowd yell.

I looked back and saw people running after me.

All of my classmates were running and yelling.

So were Mrs Brisbane and Mr Morales.

Mr Brisbane's wheelchair was almost flying.

It looked as if everyone at the fair was chasing after me.

I wanted to stop, but a hamster ball doesn't have brakes. I stopped running but the ball kept spinning. And I was spinning with it!

I rolled and rolled and rolled some more.

The trees and grass were just a blur.

I wondered how far a hamster ball could roll. Could it go on for ever?

'Come back, Humphrey!' A.J. shouted.

If I could have come back, I surely
would, because now I saw I was
rolling right toward the car park!

My heart was beating THUMPITY-
THUMP-THUMP when, all of a
sudden, the ball stopped.

It stopped so quickly, I did a triple
flip.

When I'd settled down, I looked up.

A huge foot was right on top of my
hamster ball!

Then a huge hand reached down and picked the ball up.

'Who have we got here?' the man holding the ball said.

By then, the crowd had caught up with me.

I heard Mrs Brisbane's voice say, 'Thank you for saving Humphrey, Officer Jones.'

A huge eye looked down at my hamster ball.

'I should probably give this hamster a ticket for speeding,' Police Officer Jones said. 'But I'll let him go with a warning this time.'

Everybody laughed, except me.

I was way too tired to laugh.

Richie came running up. He
looked VERY-VERY-VERY worried.

'Richie, what were you thinking?'
Mrs Brisbane asked.

'I'm sorry. I didn't think the ball
would roll away,' he said.

Then he looked down at me. 'I'm

so sorry, Humphrey. I made a big
mistake. I wouldn't want anything
bad to happen to you.'

I don't want anything bad to
happen to me, either. But I know
Richie would never want to hurt me.

★

Mrs Brisbane took me back to the stage.

Mr Morales and all my friends were waiting there.

'This has been a very surprising fair,' Mr Morales announced.

That was TRUE-TRUE-TRUE.

'Thanks to our friend Humphrey, I don't think there will ever be another fair like it,' he continued.

Everybody laughed, except Og and me. I was still too tired to laugh.

Maybe Og was tired, too.

'So, for their great signs, their terrific hamster hats, and their special classroom pets, I'm awarding the prize for best classroom spirit to

Room 26!' he said.

My tiny ears twitched with all the clapping and cheering that followed.

Then Mr Morales gave each student in Room 26 a free ticket for the bouncy castle.

As you can imagine, my friends were unsqueakably happy.

'Thanks, Humphrey,' Sayeh said.

'You're the best,' A.J. told me.

'You're Number One!' Miranda said.

Then my friends all left for castle bouncing and candy floss, for face painting and cakes.

I didn't have a ticket, but that was fine with me.

I'd had enough adventure for one day. I was ready for a nice long nap.

'Well, Og,' I said, right before I dozed off. 'Summer fairs are even more surprising than I thought. Don't you agree?'

My eyes were already closing when I heard a very loud 'BOING-BOING-BOING!'

Look for my book of
unsqueakably funny jokes

Or why not try the
puzzles and games in my
fun-fun-fun activity
book!

Puzzles and Games

From everybody's favourite hamster: ME!!

Secret Codes!

Jokes!

Puzzles!

Humphrey's
Book of
Fun-Fun-Fun

ff   Betty G. Birney

Humphrey and his friends have been hard at work making a brand new FUN-FUN-FUN website just for you!

Play Humphrey's exciting new game, share your pet pictures, find fun crafts and activities, read Humphrey's very own diary and discover all the latest news from your favourite furry friend at:

www.funwithhumphrey.com